This book belongs to

Leah

age 4

Stories
to Share

hinkler

Contents

Published by Hinkler Books Pty Ltd
45–55 Fairchild Street
Heatherton Victoria 3202 Australia
www.hinkler.com.au

Cover Design: Aimee Zumis
Cover Illustration: Gabi Murphy
Prepress: Graphic Print Group

ISBN: 978 1 7436 7815 2

Printed and bound in China

Mark Chambers

Brian is a very smelly bear,

But he doesn't seem to care.

"I smell nice!" he shouts. "I am ***clean***!"

His friends, however, are not so keen...

Cough
Cough

Some cough,
some wheeze and hold their noses tight.

His best pals, the rabbits, leap far out of sight.

But Brian doesn't seem to have a clue.

He says, "Mmmm." Others say, "Pooooh!"

Pooooh!

He smells out the bushes, he honks out the shed!

His stench would keep spiders away from your bed.

He stinks out the pond and pongs out the wood.
You'd be wise to run far away if you could!

“I smell great,” he says. “I don’t sniff.”

You wouldn’t say that if ***you*** caught a whiff!

Smell-o-grap
Smell
Jan
Year

One morning, old Badger said, "That's ***enough***!
What ***are*** we to do with that big stinky scruff?"

Hear, hear!
SMELL

"We just can't go on. He's putting us to shame.

His smell is so *awful*, but to him it seems tame."

The friends made a plan named "**MISSION: SCRUB**",
And armed themselves with soap and a tub.

“Hey Brian!” they called. “Come on over here!”

Brian looked at them puzzled, scratching his ear.

"We've found an old bath.

It's full of mud and it stinks!"

The animals all whispered,

"Well, that's what ***he*** thinks."

Brian grinned as he ran; the ultimate dash.

He leapt high as a kite, then down with a...

"This tub isn't full of stinky, smelly stuff!

It's just soapy water," Brian said in a huff.

So Brian, who smelt more than anyone you know,

More than rotten old socks and fluff on your toe...

Now smells just like flowers, and has changed his name,

To just Brian Bear, never smelly again!

I'm NOT SCARED

Dan Crisp

Lee Wildish

I'm not scared of MONSTERS.
They don't frighten me.

Even ones with **scary eyes**;

I'd have them
round for tea!

HOME SWEET
HOME

I'm not scared of GIANTS,

hanging out in the wild.

Even if they're man-eating beasts,

and I am just a child.

I'm not scared of SPIDERS,

be they as big as a bus.

Cornered by a crowd of

CROCS;

I wouldn't make a fuss.

I'm even fine with WITCHES,

as evil as they can be.

GHOSTS, GHOULS and VAMPIRES –

they don't frighten me!

I'm not scared of SKELETONS,

rattling all their bones.

Or strange sounds from the cellar;

the creepy moans and groans.

I'm not scared of OGRES and their great big beady eyes.

Lurking under bridges; they can't make me cry.

The lions

and the tigers,

great **grizzly bears** too.

They don't scare me **one little bit...**

how about you?

I'm not scared of JELLYFISH,

SHARKS or

WRIGGLING EELS.

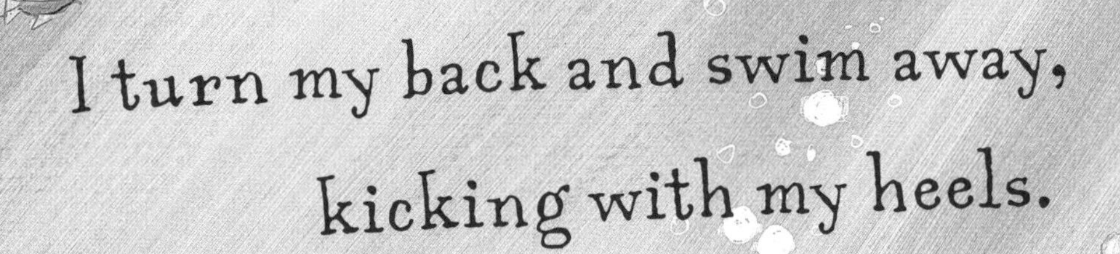

I turn my back and swim away,

kicking with my heels.

I'm not afraid of DRAGONS,

with their fire and scaly skin.

ROARING,
SCREAMING and jumping about –
all I do is grin.

I might be scared of DINOSAURS,
if they were still around.
Hang on there just a minute.
What's that
funny sound?

You'll have to please excuse me;

there's someone at the door . . .

ROAAAAAAARRRR!

It Takes Two to T'wit T'woo

Paula Knight • Guiliano Ferri

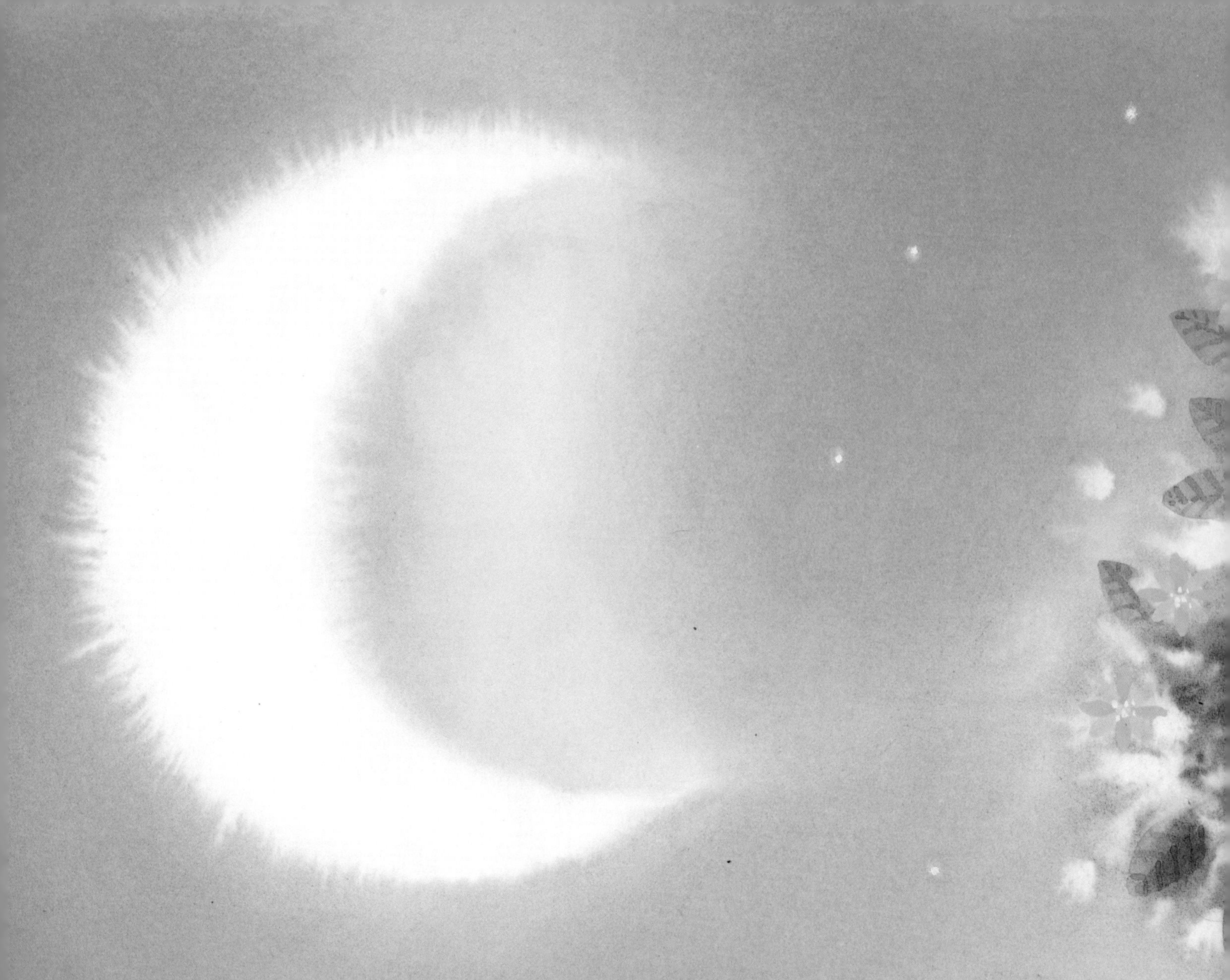

Olive Owl could only say 't'wit'.

"T'wit, t'wit," she went. She couldn't say 't'woo'.

She dearly wished to meet another owl who could hoot 't'woo', so that they could 't'wit t'woo' together.

Olive perched high up in her tree and called out,
"T'wit... T'wit..."

She listened carefully with her pointy ears.

"Ribbit... Ribbit..." came the reply.

"Who's there?" said Olive.

"I don't suppose 'ribbit' will do?" asked the frog.

"No, 'ribbit' will never do," said Olive.

She really needed a 't'woo' to go with her 't'wit'.

"T'wit... T'wit... T'wit..." called Olive, trying again.

Her pointy ears were pricked, listening carefully.

"Quack, quack! Quack, quack!" came the reply.

"Who's there?" said Olive.

“I don’t suppose a ‘quack’ will do?” asked the duck.

“I’m sorry,” said Olive, sadly. She was hoping for a ‘t’woo’.

This time, Olive shouted, **"T'wit!"** a bit louder, hoping that somewhere, someone with a lovely 't'woo' might hear her.

"GRRRRRRRRRR," came the reply.

"Who's there?" called Olive.

"I don't suppose a 'grrrrrr' will do?" asked the great big grizzly bear.

Olive sighed, "No, not at all, I'm afraid."

What she really wanted was a hooty tooty 't'woo'!

"T'wit... T'wit... T'wit, t'wit, t'wit, t'wit, t'wit!"

This time, Olive carried on 't'witting' over and over again, hoping that her dream owl would surely hear her.

"Anyone there?" she called out.

Before long, new friends surrounded Olive. Everyone had heard her 't'wits', and had come to find out what all the fuss was about. Everyone, that was, apart from Albert.

Buzzz
Squeak
Hisss
Woof

Albert lived far away, in another tree, in another wood, over the hill.

"T'WOO," he tooted. But nobody could hear him. What Albert wanted more than ever was a 't'wit' to go with his 't'woo'.

Somewhere in the distance, he thought he could hear a terrible din of quacking, oinking, growling, croaking, hissing, meowing, buzzing, squeaking and woofing. And the odd hee-haw...

Olive looked down at the duck, the cat, the donkey, the frog, the dog, the snake, the bee, the pig, the mouse and the great big grizzly bear.

"What will you do if you can't find a 't'woo'?" they asked.

"I don't know. Please can you help me?" said Olive.

Together, they all took a huge deep breath...

"T'wi-i-i-t!"

they shouted at the
tops of their voices.

They hushed and listened for a reply. Sure enough, from a far-away wood over the hill, someone had heard them…

"T'woo... T'woo-hoo!" hooted Albert, hardly able to believe what he was hearing.

"T'wi-i-i-t!"

There it was again!

Albert was excited and set off in the direction of the 't'wit', calling, **"T'WOOO!"** as he flew.

Albert landed on the tree, right next to her. They had found each other at last.

"T'woo!" he said.

"T'wit!" said Olive.

"GRRRRR," said the great big grizzly bear. "That's the wrong way round!"

"T'wit... T'woo!"
said Olive and Albert,
one after the other.

The animals cheered.
Olive and Albert continued
't'witting' and 't'wooing'
together until dawn, when
they snuggled up for a
well-earned sleep.

The Beast Beneath the Bed

Clemency Pearce

Laura Hughes

Each night when warmly snuggled down, when dreams are swirling in my head,

There comes a creepy, crawling noise...

...THE BEAST BENEATH THE BED!

The scratchy sounds and little growls echo in the dark.

I pull the covers to my chin and hear him cough and bark.

One day, I snuck a little peek, and saw the fearsome brute.

He was two-feet high, with bright red eyes. Anything but cute!

With tangled fur and awesome fangs, he really was a sight.

His claws were long and razor sharp; he gave me such a fright!

I watched, as he began to steal all my lovely toys.

He ate my smartest pair of shoes, then made
a burping noise.

BURRRPP!!!

He tore right up the bookcase on lightning little paws.

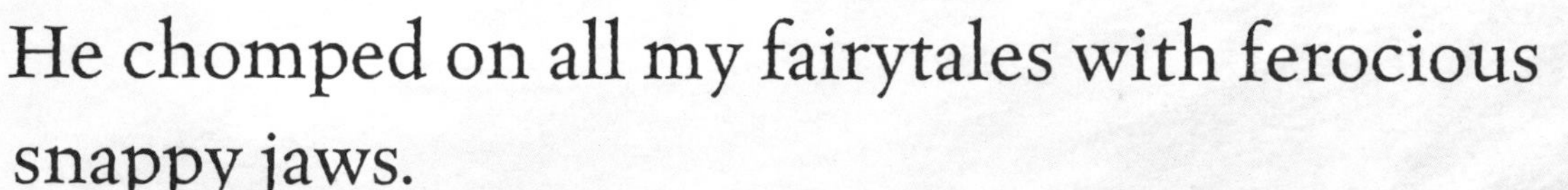

He chomped on all my fairytales with ferocious snappy jaws.

He swung upon my lampshade,

“WHEEEEEEEEEEEEEE!”,

howling as he flew.

I'd never seen such naughtiness! My horror grew and grew.

Then he fell down,

'BUMP!',

and left a dent upon the floor.

He gobbled up my teddy bear...

... **THAT** was the final straw!

"STOP IT NOW, YOU FIEND!"

I yelled, leaping to my feet.

"YOU'VE MESSED UP ALL MY PRECIOUS THINGS AND I LIKE TO KEEP THEM NEAT!"

At this the creature froze and stared. He was scared of me instead!

I found my fear had disappeared of The Beast Beneath The Bed.

"Why are **YOU** so terrified? So petrified?" I said.

He replied, quite mystified,

"You're The Beast Above My Head!"

"When the sun shines bright and clear, and I'm snoozing in my den,

You ruin all my magic mess by cleaning up again!"

We had both been naughty monsters, in very different ways.

He'd sabotaged my night-times...

and I'd haunted all his days.

So we put our heads together, and we made a special deal.

I'd let him play with all my toys, if he promised not to steal.

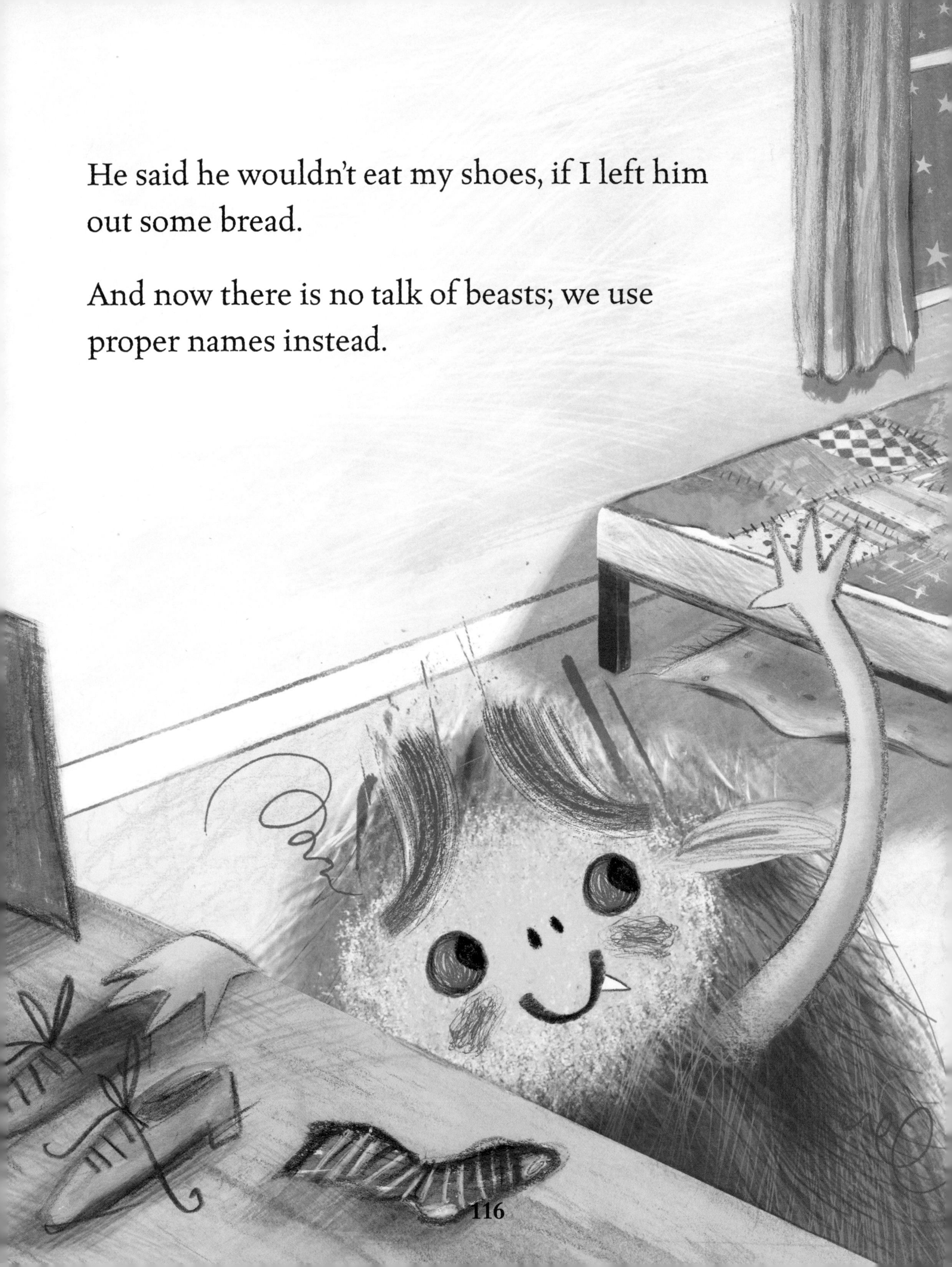

He said he wouldn't eat my shoes, if I left him out some bread.

And now there is no talk of beasts; we use proper names instead.

So when I'm drifting off at night, and hear those scratchy snarls,

I just say,

"MORNING, ROBERT!",

and he says,

"GOODNIGHT, CHARLES!"

Roble's Rain Dance

Paula Knight • Gavin Scott

Roble is hot and thirsty. It hasn't rained in his desert for a long time.

Roble shares a burrow with many other gerbils. During the day, it gives them shelter from the burning sun and hungry swooping eagles. Every gerbil has their very own entrance hole.

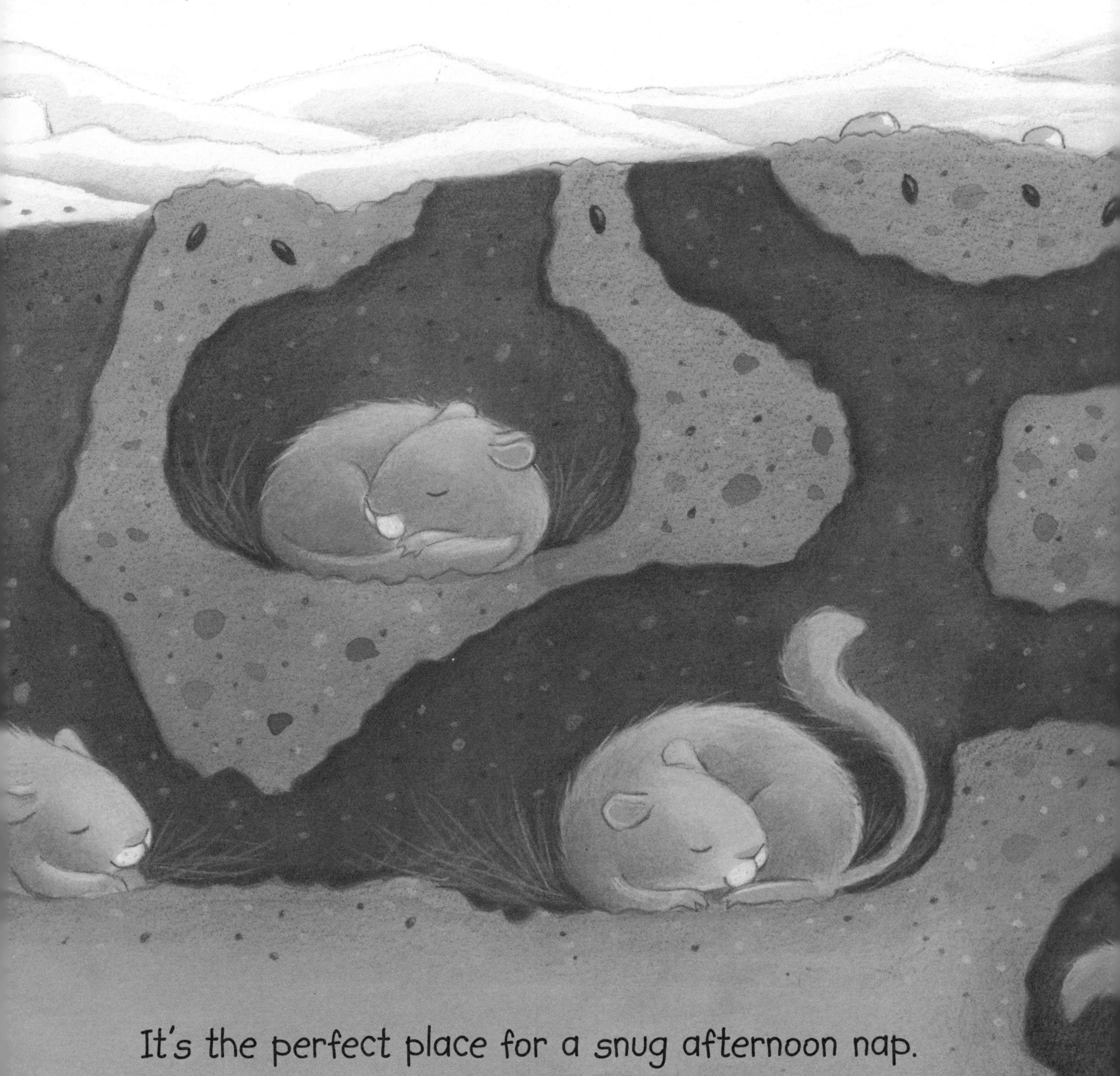

It's the perfect place for a snug afternoon nap.

At night, Roble searches for food. He bumps into Juba gerbil, who lives in the hole next door.

"Not much to eat tonight," says Juba. "Only curled-up crusty old cactus leaves!"

So they scurry to the next plant instead.

"Where are all the prickly pear fruits?" says Roble.

"What are we to do?" cries Juba.

I'm still hungry!

I couldn't find much to eat at all. Only these dried-up seeds, and they taste horrid!

The gazelles ate all the aloe!

The cactus is all crusty!

The prickly pear was all but bare!

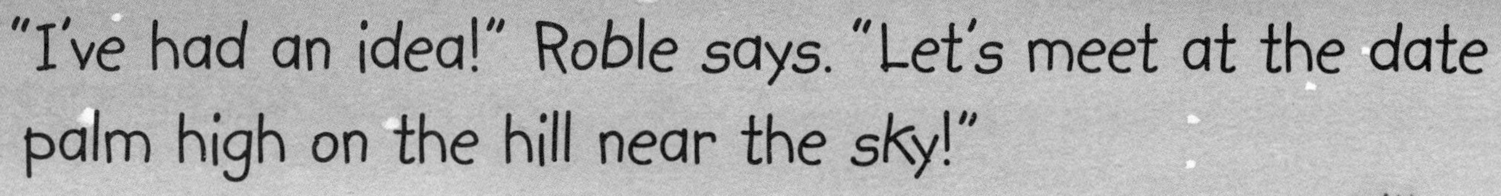

"I've had an idea!" Roble says. "Let's meet at the date palm high on the hill near the sky!"

The gerbils march past the *bare* prickly pear, around the crusty cactus and the *barren* aloe...

...up the big hill over the dry dusty earth to the date palm at the top.

"We must perform a rain dance for the sky by pittering and pattering our feet on the earth, like the sound of rain."

High on the hill where the *sky* can *see* them, the gerbils hold hands.

They begin to sing and dance.

"Rain, rain, come to stay,

Come to visit us today!

Rain, rain, fall and pour,

Sprinkle on the desert floor."

Pitter-patter, pitter-patter go their tiny feet.

"Rain, rain, pitter-patter,

Feed the cactus, make it fatter!

Rain, rain, and cloud-burst,

Shower us and quench our thirst."

Round and round they dance and chant until they flop to the floor, exhausted.

Splosh!
Plop!

Splish!

Splash!

"Wake up!" cries Roble. "Our rain dance has worked!"

Hooray!

Later that day, beautiful flowers bloom all over the desert.

The gerbils are so happy that they want to reward Roble for helping to bring the rain. They celebrate by crowning him 'Rain King'.

There is enough for everybody to eat and drink, with plenty left over...

...for splishing and splashing in cool muddy puddles!

'Roble' is a Somali name meaning 'born during the rainy season'. Somalia is a country in East Africa.